BOB

Tracey Campbell Pearson

A SUNBURST BOOK
FARRAR, STRAUS AND GIROUX

Bob, a rooster, lived with a bunch of chickens. The chickens clucked all day long, and so did Bob: "Cluck, cluck, cluck."

One day Henrietta told him the truth. "Bob," she said, "you are not a chicken. You are a rooster. You need to stop clucking and learn how to crow so you can wake up the girls every morning. That's what roosters do."

"Will you teach me?" asked Bob.
"No," said Henrietta. "I am a cat. Cats don't crow. I can only teach you how to meow."

So Bob learned how to meow.
Then he went off in search of a rooster.

MEOW-MEOW

Bob walked and walked until he met a dog.
He learned how to woof and wag.
But a dog is not a rooster, so Bob continued down the road.

MEOW-MEOW
WOOF-WAG

Bob walked and walked until he found a pond full of frogs.
He learned how to ribbet and hop.
But a frog is not a rooster, so Bob continued down the road.

MEOW-MEOW
WOOF-WAG
RIBBET-RIBBET-HOP-HOP

Bob walked and walked until he came to a field of cows.
He learned how to moo and tried to chew his cud.
Except he didn't have one.
Bob decided to eat bugs instead.

But a cow is not a rooster, so Bob continued down the road with a belly full of bugs.

MEOW-MEOW
WOOF-WAG
RIBBET-RIBBET-HOP-HOP
MOOOOOO
YUM-YUM-BUGS

He walked right out of the day and into the night, searching for a rooster to teach him how to crow.

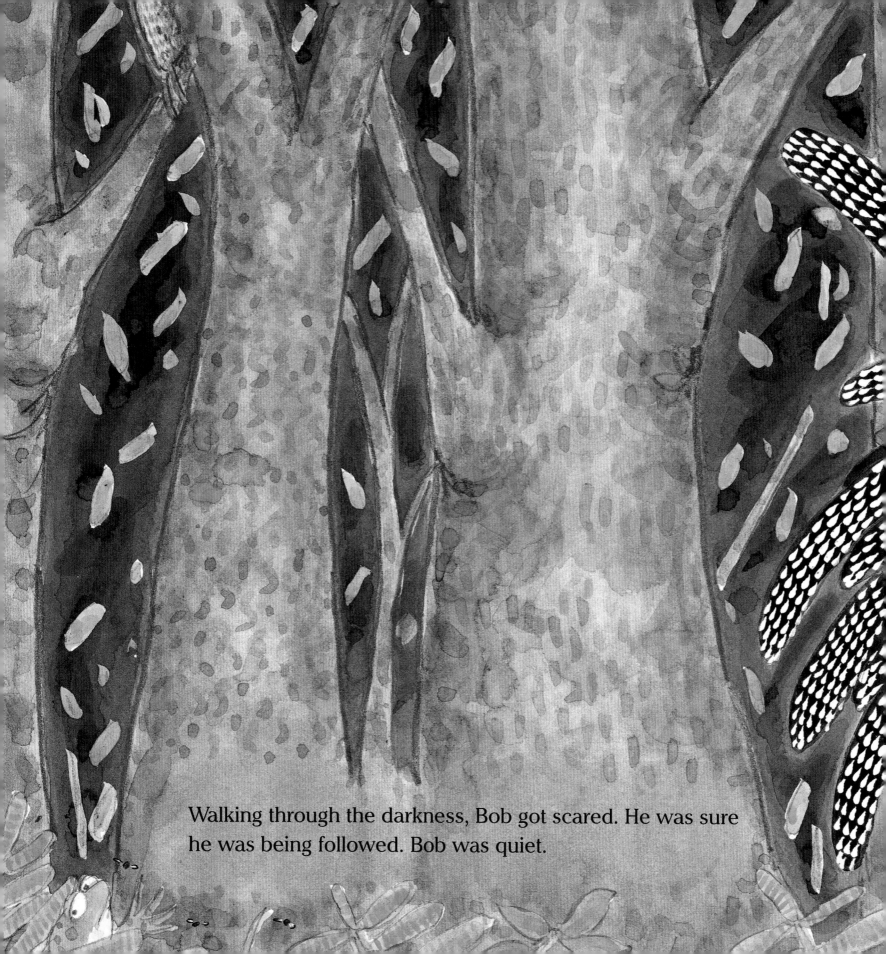

Walking through the darkness, Bob got scared. He was sure
he was being followed. Bob was quiet.

Then a stranger called out, "Whooo? Whooo? Whooo?"
Not wanting to be rude, Bob whispered, "Bob, Bob, Bob."
Again the stranger asked, "Whooo? Whooo? Whooo?"
And again Bob whispered, "Bob, Bob, Bob."
And so it went all night long, over and over again. Until the
first morning light, when Bob heard . . .

"Cock-a

"doodle-do!"

There in the middle of the road was a bird who looked a lot like Bob. His name was Fred, and he taught Bob how to crow.

It was dark by the time Bob walked all the way home.
He settled in for the night, being careful not to wake the
girls or Henrietta.

Bob was too excited to sleep, so he was wide awake when the fox came. He let out a big

"Cock-a-doodle-do!"

But it didn't scare the fox.

Then Bob called out a loud

"Meow-Meow-M

Woof-Woo

Ribbe

Mooooo

ow

Woof

Ribbet-Ribbet

Yum-Yum-Fox!"

The fox, terrified and amazed by all the animals in the coop,
especially the one that sounded hungry for fox,
ran home, never to return.

And from then on, every morning Bob woke the girls and Henrietta up with a

"Cock-a

Or if he felt like it, a

"Meow-Woof

Ribbet-Moooo Yum-Yum-Bugs!"

Distributed in Canada by Douglas & McIntyre Ltd.

Printed in the United States of America

First edition, 2002

Sunburst edition, 2006

1 3 5 7 9 10 8 6 4 2

Library of Congress Cataloging-in-Publication Data

Pearson, Tracey Campbell.

Bob / Tracey Campbell Pearson.

p.   cm.

Summary: While looking for someone to teach him how to crow, a rooster learns to sound like many different animals and finds that his new skills come in handy.

ISBN-13: 978-0-374-40871-8 (pbk.)

ISBN-10: 0-374-40871-8 (pbk.)

[1. Roosters—Fiction.   2. Animal sounds—Fiction.   3. Animals—Fiction.   4. Humorous stories.]   I. Title.

PZ7.P323318 Bo 2002

[E]—dc21

2001040439

For Jean